Puppy Mudge
Loves His Blanket

By Cynthia Rylant

Illustrated by Isidre Mones

in the style of Suçie Stevenson

READY-TO-READ

SIMON & SCHUSTER BOOKS FOR YOUNG READERS

New York   London   Toronto   Sydney   Singapore

SIMON & SCHUSTER BOOKS FOR YOUNG READERS
An imprint of Simon & Schuster Children's Publishing Division
1230 Avenue of the Americas, New York, New York 10020
Text copyright © 2004 by Cynthia Rylant
Illustrations copyright © 2004 by Suçie Stevenson
SIMON & SCHUSTER BOOKS FOR YOUNG READERS is a trademark of
Simon & Schuster, Inc.
READY-TO-READ is a registered trademark of Simon & Schuster, Inc.
Book design by Mark Siegel
The text for this book is set in Goudy.
The illustrations are rendered in pen-and-ink and watercolor.
Manufactured in the United States of America
10 9 8 7 6 5 4 3 2 1
CIP data for this book is available from the Library of Congress.
ISBN 0-689-83983-9

This is Mudge.
He is Henry's puppy.

Mudge has a blanket.

Mudge LOVES his blanket.

He sleeps on it.

He hides under it.

He takes it places.

Sometimes he loses it.

Where is Mudge's blanket now?

Henry looks on the chair.

Mudge looks on the chair.
No blanket.

Henry looks under the bed.
Mudge looks under the bed.

No blanket.

Mudge is so sleepy.
He needs his blanket.

Mudge sniffs.

He sniffs and sniffs and sniffs.

Good Mudge!
He sniffed all the way . . .

to his blanket!

Now he can rest.